Aria and the Magic Apron

Aria and the Magic Apron

Pooja Dhingra
and
Stuti Agarwal

JUGGERNAUT BOOKS
C-I-128, First Floor, Sangam Vihar, Near Holi Chowk,
New Delhi 110080, India

First published by Juggernaut Books 2025

Copyright © Pooja Dhingra 2025

10 9 8 7 6 5 4 3 2 1

P-ISBN: 9789353454203
E-ISBN: 9789353459147

This is a work of fiction. Any resemblance to persons, living or dead, or to actual incidents is purely coincidental.

All rights reserved. No part of this publication may be reproduced, transmitted or stored in a retrieval system in any form or by any means without the written permission of the publisher.

Typeset in Adobe Caslon Pro by R. Ajith Kumar, Noida

Printed at Thomson Press India Ltd

To the younger us,
the magic was always in you.

Contents

1. A Sunday Brownie — 1
2. The Baking Competition — 13
3. Let the Baking Begin — 21
4. The Magic Apron — 35
5. On a Roll — 45
6. Toasts, Tumbles and Torn Threads — 63
7. Shattered Shells — 79
8. It Might Just Be a Comeback — 93

1

A Sunday Brownie

'AAAAAAAHHHHHHHHH!' Aria screeched.

'I'm not done! I'm not done!' she shouted, flinging a wild quarter teaspoon of salt and a whole cup of baking soda into the swirling chocolate chaos of her Gooey Choco-Love Brownie batter. Her whisk was moving at warp speed, splattering cocoa lava across the counter.

'Peanut, no! Get away from the bowl!' she barked, nudging her beagle with one batter-smeared knee. The dog gave her a look that said, *Just one lick, please,* and resumed orbiting her like a sugar-craving satellite.

From the kitchen counter, Pari Doshi's sunny voice floated out of the iPad speaker. 'If you're just joining, don't worry! You can rewind later. Right now, set aside your batter and grease your tins – let's make baking magic!'

'Papa! I need backup! There are egg shells in the batter!' Aria yelled, waving her spatula like a flag of distress.

'Coming, coming!' Mr Mehra bustled over, apron flecked with golden crumbs. 'Had to finish frying the chicken for the katsu curry – here, hand me the bowl. You butter the tin.'

Relief washed over Aria. She wiped her chocolate-covered fingers on her hair without a second thought, curls now streaked with cocoa. Her red apron, dotted with tiny cherry cupcakes, looked like it had survived a dessert hurricane. Her T-shirt of the day read 'Sprinkle Queen' in glittery purple, and her eyes sparkled like molten chocolate chips.

'Alright, bakers, oven time! See you in twenty-four minutes for the gooiest brownies of your life. Don't forget to tag me – @PariDoesDessert!' Pari chimed.

Aria high-fived her dad. 'Nice job, team!'

'Pea Pea, you can lick up the batter now,' she said.

'Hey, me too!' her father protested.

'Oops! Sorry, Dad!' Aria laughed.

Peanut woofed, rushing to steal the bowl.

'Fine. I'll just settle for the chocolate chips,' Dad said, popping a ton of them in his mouth.

'Mum, can we see what photos we can upload for today? You think PD will see our bake this time?' PD, AKA Pari Doshi, only the best dessert chef in the world there ever was.

'Let's manifest it,' Mrs Mehra smiled, typing rapidly on her laptop. 'I've got some great clips too. Come, we'll pick the cutest ones.'

'Mmm … this looks cute!' Aria said, scrolling through the pictures. 'Oh my god, Pea's tongue is fully in the bowl – iconic!'

'Ye—'

'OH MY GOD!'

Mr Mehra's scream sent both mother and daughter running to the kitchen.

But they didn't have to go all the way to see the train of liquid, foaming, burnt-but-still-

bubbling batter spilling out of the oven and onto the floor in a lava-like puddle.

'Stand back,' Mr Mehra said, opening the oven door carefully.

The brownies looked ... furious! The batter was still frothing and fizzing over, a pungent smell taking over the room, sending even Peanut to bury himself under the covers in the bedroom.

'What happened?' Mrs Mehra wondered.

'I don't know. I'm sure I followed the recipe,' Mr Mehra insisted. 'Let me check. Yes ... I did that ... Yes ... I did *that* ... Aru, you added a quarter teaspoon of salt?'

'Yes,' Aria nodded.

'And one teaspoon of baking soda, right?'

She froze.

'I ... I added a cup,' she whispered, her eyes welling up.

'What?' the parents said together.

'A cup! I thought it said one cup of baking soda!'

There was silence. Then laughter. Her parents pulled her into a tight hug.

'A classic mistake!' Mr Mehra grinned.

'Don't worry, we'll make another batch. PD will never know,' Mrs Mehra comforted her.

'We could even add fun flavours to it! Sabina, help us clean up while we prep for round two?'

From the screen, Pari's voice returned. 'That's twenty-four minutes! Your brownies should be gooey, glorious and ready for a scoop of ice cream. By the way, loving all the photos you're tagging me on. Remember – a random pick will get my personalized goodie bag. For now, make sure to have fun with it – do a little dance!

Aria burst into tears again. 'Another weekend she won't see my bake!'

'She will! We'll get another batch in the next

thirty minutes, beta,' Mr Mehra said. 'And we always have next Sunday. What does PD say?'

'Have fun with baking,' Aria said softly.

'Exactly. And how about we go get a stick of your favourite PD's chikoo–hazelnut kulfi after dinner today?'

Aria managed a small smile. 'Okay … maybe a double stick.'

How to crack an egg

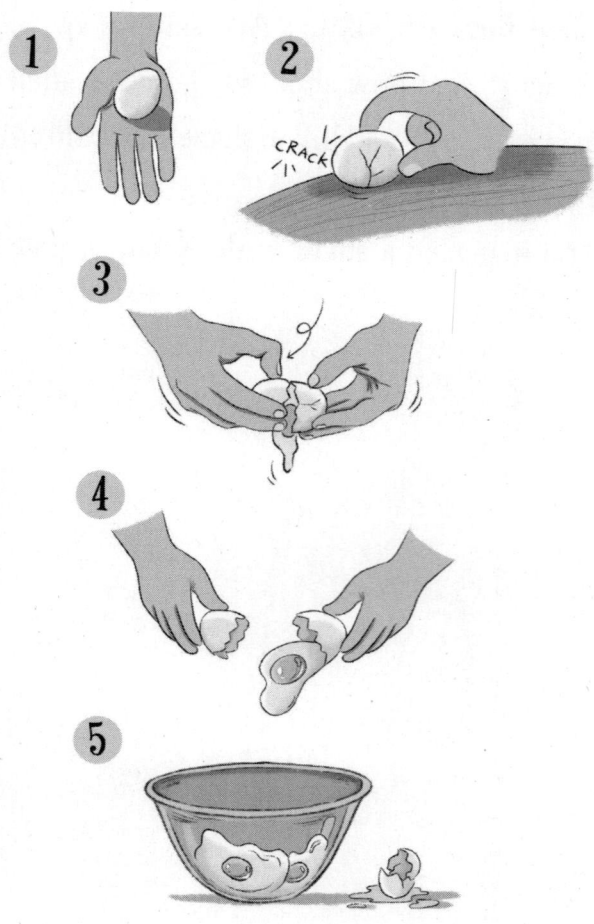

2

The Baking Competition

'I swear she said Pari Doshi,' Aria whispered.

'What?' Sarah said, louder than necessary.

'Sshhh,' Aria nudged. 'We'll miss it.'

'Oh, *you* shush.' Sarah raised her hand. 'Ma'am, did you say Pari Doshi will be judging the baking competition?'

Apart from being quite the school football legend and a close contender to the world record for the most *Moana* rewatches, Sarah was also Aria's best friend in the whole wide world ... and the complete opposite of her. To begin with, she was never one to sit quiet.

'Yes, Sarah. Now, if you'd just listen – ' Miss Nanda, the school Home Science teacher (and a baking wiz) said.

'Don't roll your eyes ... don't roll your eyes,' Aria whispered to Sarah.

'Sorry,' Sarah said, batting her big brown eyes and trying hard not to smile.

Miss Nanda pressed on. 'So yes, for the first time ever, Mary Theresa's is going to have a baking competition. Four rounds. A grand finale with Pari Doshi herself! What do you win? A summer internship at her bakery and a chance to feature your own flavoured cupcake in Pari's signature box!'

The Baking Competition

'Woah!' Aria gasped.

Miss Nanda let the gasps and hoots subside before continuing. 'So that is it. Add your names to the list if you would like to be part of it. I want serious bakers only. Tanya, bring me the list by lunch.'

The room exploded into chatter the second Miss Nanda left.

'There is no way you are not signing up,' Sarah exclaimed, spinning towards Aria.

'I don't know, it's going to be so hard. And I won't have Papa there.'

'Oh my god, Aru. Stop thinking! You are so annoying. Just do it, will you, so I can get more of your yummy bakes, please.'

'Sarah, you could bake the same things!'

'Ya, not really. I only joined the class because of you. And because I need some sugar in my life. Mum and Dad are treating Junior Football like it's the Olympics,' Sarah made a fake sad face.

Aria giggled.

'Also, it is Pari Doshi. You talk about her nonstop and how you would like to be her and what not. Just do it now. I promise I'll help. And I'm actually sure you will be fab at it! I'm telling Uncle–Aunty if you don't.'

'Okay, okay,' Aria said. 'Calm down. Doing it now.'

Sarah didn't leave her friend's

side until she signed up. And even though Aria was quite scared about doing it all alone, Sarah was right – there was no way she was going to miss a chance of meeting – and baking with (fingers crossed) – PD! Can you even imagine!

How to fold and mix cake batter

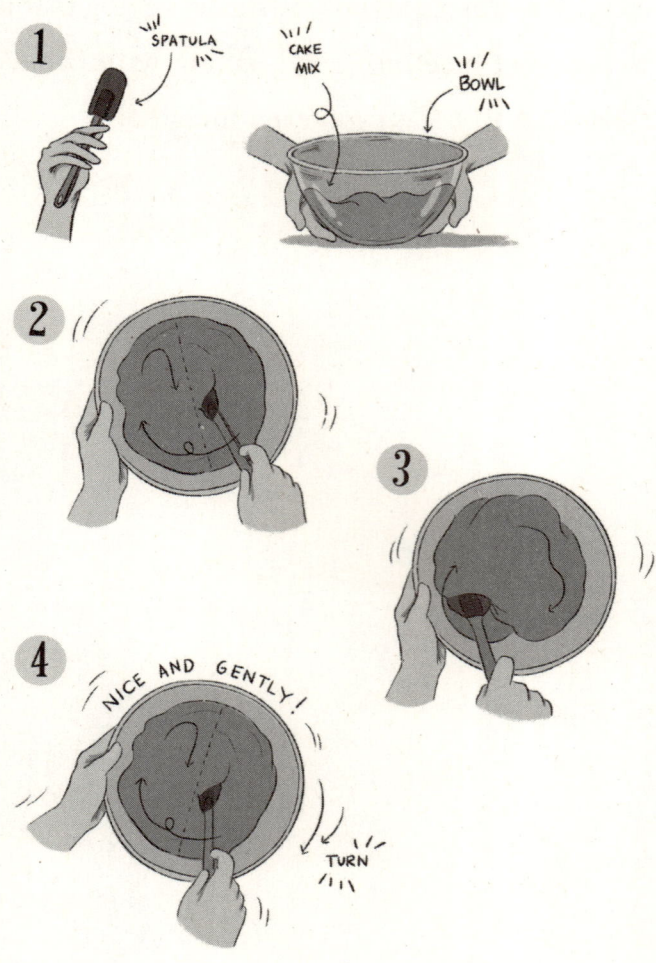

3

Let the Baking Begin

Tarts.

That was the brief for the first round. Just one word. It felt like a puzzle more than a tip really.

'How about an apple and caramelized tomato ketchup tart?' Sarah suggested. 'Can you aramelize tomato ketchup?'

'Bye, Sarah!' Aria groaned.

'You don't eat apples with tomato ketchup?'

'No. Because I'm sane. Anyway, I'm thinking something classic.'

'Classics are overrated,' Sarah sniffed. 'But fine, Miss Predictable. What's your genius plan?'

'Chocolate ganache tart. Simple. Elegant. Can't go wrong.'

And in Aria's head, she saw it: a crumbly, buttery pastry; a dark glossy chocolate ganache that's just the right amount of airy. Her first solo bake had to be perfect – and that meant keeping it simple and focused.

'Okay, that does sound pretty amazing. Dibs on it! I get the whole tart after the tasting. You better pack it somehow and give it to me.'

'Done.'

On the day of the competition, Aria was ready. Well, almost.

She stared down at her station like it was a battlefield. Ingredients? Check. Recipe? Papa's

annotated list in bold, block letters. Apron tied, hair up.

I can do this. She told herself. *I can do this.*

Miss Nanda's voice cut through the air.

'Alright, you'll have seventy-five minutes to do this. Begin!'

Aria moved fast. Flour, icing sugar, cubes of chilled butter, egg yolks (with a few bits of shells!) and a splash of cold water. Her hands knew the motions: pinch, mix, knead – until dough came together like soft clay.

Let the Baking Begin

Now for the magic: chocolate ganache.

She poured hot cream over chopped Dairy Milk Silk (Papa's tip – 'smoother than chips, trust me'), waited two beats, then stirred. It melted into a velvet swirl.

She dipped a spoon, licked.

Yum. But something was missing.

Salt. PD did that with her bakes sometimes.

A pinch. Another taste.

Mmm! Still ... something more.

Her eyes darted to the ingredients shelf – and then she sprinted.

Chilli powder!

She stirred a dash into the ganache.

'What are you doing, Aria?' Miss Nanda had appeared beside her.

Aria froze. 'Umm ... trying something?'

Miss Nanda took a lick before Aria could stop her.

'Oooh, that's clever,' she said, smiling.

Aria beamed. *Thank you, PD.* (It was her lemon chilli cookies that had planted the seed.)

'Thirty minutes left!' Miss Nanda called.

Let the Baking Begin

Back to business.

Dough out. Roll to 2 mm – Papa's voice echoed in her head. She lined the tart tin, trimmed the edges, pricked the base.

Time check: twenty minutes. She hesitated.

I'll save time. Ganache in, then bake.

She piped the silky filling in, slid it into the oven, then paced in front of it like a nervous sous chef.

Countdown mode.

Seventeen minutes.

Twelve.

Seven.

Ding!

Time to take it out.

Beautiful, she thought. A little puffed around the edges, the ganache smooth and shiny. The chilli had darkened the colour – like it *knew* it had attitude.

Aria took a deep breath. All she had to do now was lift it out of the tin, place it on the presentation board, and boom – round one, done.

She reached for the tart tin and tried to loosen the tart out of it.

Something was wrong. It wouldn't budge.

But why?

She thought about everything she had done.

Her heart skipped.

It wasn't what she had done. It was what she hadn't – buttered the tin.

Not a drop. Not even a spray of grease.

It'll still come out, she told herself in panic. *It has to.*

She wedged a knife gently under the edge and pressed a little more. The edge gave way – *crack.* A shard of crust broke off.

No, no, no ...

She tried the other side. This time, the ganache wobbled dangerously, reminding her that she had done yet another thing wrong – the ganache had to be piped later, cold.

It's fine. She steadied it with one hand, prodded again, and tried to wiggle the base out.

It clung on stubbornly.

She nudged harder. The tart cracked down the middle, chocolate oozing out like lava onto the floor.

Aria let out a small, pitiful squeak.

Five minutes to go.

Now she wasn't trying to free it anymore – she was *attacking.* Jabbing. Pulling. Scraping at it like it was gum on her shoes.

Let go. Just let go.

And then –

Clatter.

The entire tin slipped from her grip.

It flipped, spun in the air and splattered onto the floor.

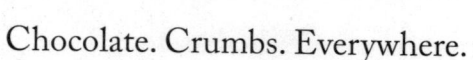

Chocolate. Crumbs. Everywhere.

She stared. Someone gasped behind her.

'I … I'll fix it,' she muttered. 'I can fix it …'

But there was no time. No tart. Nothing she could present.

'One minute left, bakers! One minute!' Miss Nanda announced, walking back into the class.

Aria didn't wait.

She tore off her apron, grabbed her bag and ran.

The chocolate smudges on her hands felt like proof that she'd tried – and failed. Again.

How to make a basic tart base

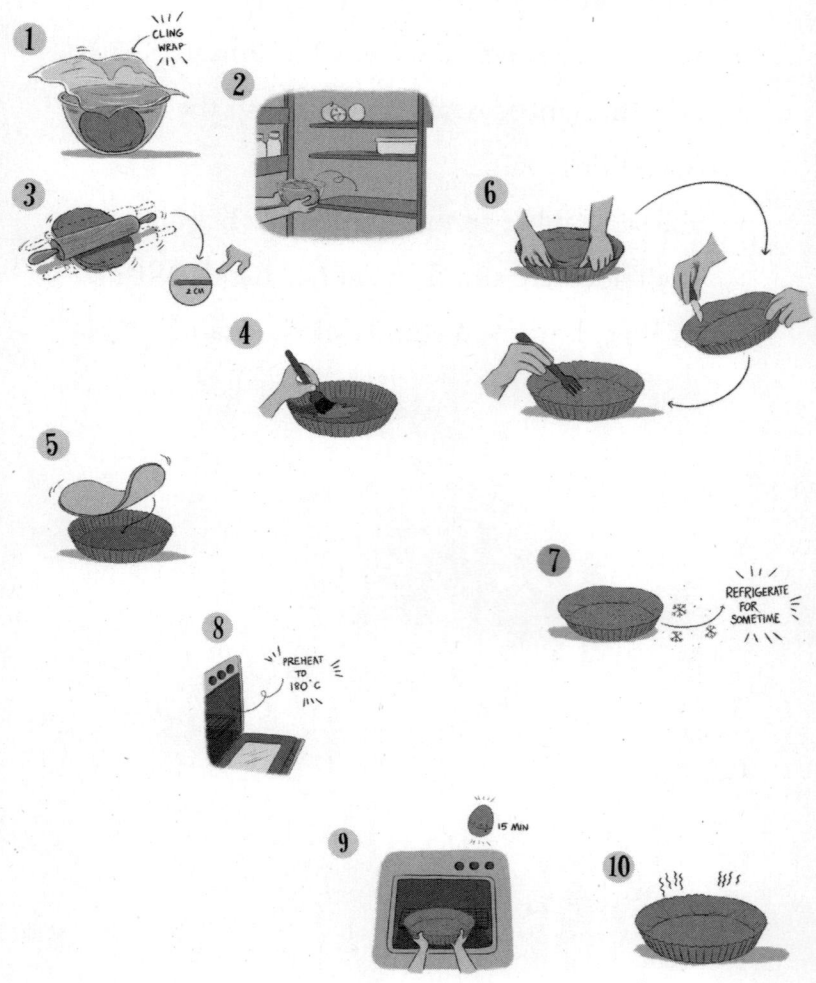

4

The Magic Apron

Aria burst through the front door, eyes stinging, cheeks streaked with tears. Her backpack thudded to the floor like a failed soufflé.

Mr Mehra looked up from the kitchen. 'Aria?'

Mrs Mehra appeared from the hallway, laptop still in hand. 'What happened?'

Aria shook her head, lips pressed tight. If she spoke, the tears would come harder.

Mr Mehra set down the carrot he was peeling and crouched to her. 'Was it the tart?'

She gave a tiny nod, and then all of it came rushing out in a messy, tearful stream: the ganache on the floor, the crust on the tin and the realization that she was the worst baker ever.

'I'm a terrible baker,' she sniffled. 'I ruined everything.'

Mrs Mehra sat down beside her and tucked a loose strand of hair behind Aria's ear. 'Sweetheart, even the best bakers have bad days. Remember that time Papa tried to make marshmallows and glued our blender shut?'

'Hey!' Mr Mehra protested. 'That was … an experiment.'

Aria gave a wet, reluctant smile.

'Tell you what,' he said, getting to his feet. 'We're going on a picnic.'

'A picnic?' Aria blinked. 'Now?'

'Right now. Emergency picnic. Stat. I'll make cheese and olive sandwiches, and Mum can pack those leftover chocolate chip cookies.'

Mrs Mehra nodded. 'And lemonade. With mint and a dash of lime, the way you like it.'

They drove out to their usual spot by the sea, where the waves hit lightly and the air smelled like sunshine and sweet earth. Mr Mehra laid out the blanket, Mrs Mehra handed Aria a sandwich, and for a while, they just sat.

Aria tore small bites from her sandwich, slowly chewing. The soft bread, the gooey cheese, those salty olives – her favourite snack.

The Magic Apron

Mr Mehra rustled in the picnic basket again. 'I was saving this for your next bake sale, but it feels like the right time.'

He pulled out a bundle wrapped in brown paper, tied with a purple ribbon and handed it to Aria.

She opened it gently, curious – and gasped.

It was the brightest, most ridiculously pretty apron she'd ever seen. A pop of pink, with a whisk that sparkled when it caught the sunlight.

'It's magic,' Mr Mehra said, eyes twinkling.

'Magic?' Aria echoed, doubtfully.

'Completely. Tested and approved by me and Mum. But it only works if you activate it.'

'How?' she asked, tentative, half smiling.

'You have to wear it and say the words. Out loud,' Mr Mehra added, handing over a piece of paper.

Aria raised an eyebrow. 'You guys don't actually believe this is magic … right?'

Mrs Mehra smiled. 'What we do believe is *you* are magic. And when you wear the apron – well ...'

Aria hesitated, fingers brushing the sparkly whisk stitched across the front.

'You don't have to believe it's real,' Mr Mehra said. 'Just ... try it. For us.'

She looked at their hopeful faces. A part of her really wanted to roll her eyes. Another part – the tired, sad one – wanted to believe them, just a little bit. Maybe wearing something silly and bright could help.

She sighed, then slipped it over her head.

'Okay,' she said, standing up slowly. 'But I'm only doing this for you two.'

She held the paper up and read out, not too loudly, not too soft:

'I am magic, and I am the best baker in the whole wide world.'

Nothing happened.

No sparkle. No swirl of stardust.

But somehow, she felt ... a little different.

Mrs Mehra clapped. Mr Mehra whooped like she'd just won a baking championship.

'Sometimes, it helps to wear your courage on the outside,' Mrs Mehra said, gently.

Aria looked down at the sparkly whisk and smiled, still uncertain, but lighter than before.

'I'm going to bake again,' she said, quietly but clearly.

'Good,' Mr Mehra said, reaching for a cookie.

Aria took one too, broke off a piece and popped it into her mouth. Sweet. Chewy. A little crunchy around the edges.

Maybe not magic.

But maybe – hope.

How to make choclate ganache

5
On a Roll

Aria stared at the apron.

Bright pink. Sparkly sequins. A glittery whisk stitched across the front like it was about to cast a sugary spell. Honestly, it looked like something

from Sarah's dress-up box – meant for princesses and tea parties, not serious bakers. Not someone trying to fix a baking disaster.

She huffed. 'This is silly,' she muttered. 'Aprons don't do magic.'

Still … she hadn't been able to stop thinking about PD.

PD, with her fearless flavours and flour-dusted nose. PD, who'd once baked a seven-layer rainbow roulade after tripping over a dog and dropping her mixing bowl. All on TV! She never gave up. She just laughed, cleaned the mess and kept going. And she always said: 'Baking comes from the heart – but a little help never hurt.'

Even she had her lucky spoon.

Aria bit her lip. *What if…*

She stepped into the school kitchen and glanced around, half-expecting someone to laugh at her. But everyone was busy with their own prepping.

Quickly, before she could change her mind, she slipped the apron over her head.

It fit perfectly. Like it had always belonged to her.

She tied it tight around her waist, heart thudding, and whispered the words her parents had taught her:

'I am magic. And I am the best baker in the whole wide world.'

She held her breath.

Nothing.

No lightning. No sparkles. No dramatic swirl of flour rising in the air.

Aria exhaled with a groan. 'Figures.'

But as she walked up to her work station, her sneakers squeaking against the tiles, something felt … different. Not loud or flashy. Just a quiet shift. A strange lightness in her chest.

She didn't feel nervous.

Her hands weren't shaking. Her stomach wasn't flopping like a soufflé in a windstorm.

Instead, it felt like the air itself had changed – it was thinner, fizzier, like breathing in bubbles. The apron around her waist felt warmer than usual, as if it had caught some fairy dust just for her. It hugged her gently, not tight, but snug in that perfect way a grown-up's arms sometimes were – steadying and safe.

This round's challenge: cheesecake.

Aria blinked at the ingredients laid out in front of her. Without overthinking it, she knew what she wanted to make.

Pineapple and black pepper cheesecake.

Weird? Absolutely.

On a Roll

But pineapple was her favourite fruit. And she remembered trying it once at a street cart, sprinkled with black pepper. It had zinged and zapped her tastebuds like a tiny lightning bolt. She'd never forgotten it.

She gathered her ingredients.

First step: eggs.

Egg cracking had always been her nemesis. She winced

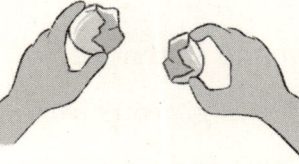

as she picked one up. This was where things usually went wrong – shell bits, gooey fingers, mild panic. But she tapped it against the side of the bowl and –

Plop.

Perfect.

No shell shards.

Her eyes widened. She cracked another.

Plop. Perfect again.

She blinked at the bowl.

Was it the apron? Was it her?

The sequins on the front seemed to wink back at her. She narrowed her eyes at the apron, half-suspicious, half-delighted. 'You and me, huh?' she whispered. The apron didn't reply but the butter melted just a little quicker after that.

She didn't know what it was. But she wasn't going to stop now.

With growing excitement, she crushed biscuits and stirred them into warm butter,

On a Roll

pressing them into the base of her tin with practised confidence. The cream cheese filling came next — fluffy, just sweet enough, blended with the whisked eggs, pineapple purée and a careful pinch of black pepper.

Just a pinch. Like a spell.

She tasted a spoonful. Her eyebrows flew up.

Yes!

Into the oven it went. While it baked, she sliced

fresh pineapple into thin, delicate rings and arranged them in a blooming swirl over the baked cake. It looked like sunshine caught on a plate.

When Miss Nanda took a bite, she paused mid-chew.

Then she nodded slowly.

'Delightfully strange,' she said. 'And I mean that in the best way.'

Aria didn't win the round, but she got a shiny 'Highly Commended for Flavour Bravery' sticker. And somehow, that felt better than gold.

Because she'd trusted herself. And that felt pretty huge.

★

On a Roll

Time for round three: choux pastry.

The kind of bake that sank if you so much as looked at it wrong.

Aria tried to calm her nerves. She wanted to believe the apron. She wanted to believe in herself so bad.

HIGHLY COMMENDED FOR FLAVOUR BRAVERY

The last bake had gone so well. And she had done it. It had to be something – the apron, her even. But she didn't have the time to do that now. She had to do what she had to do.

She thought of PD as she tied her apron and whispered the words again, still unsure, but with a smile: 'I am magic. And I am the best baker in the whole wide world.'

This time, she didn't just say the words. She *felt* them. Like they came from somewhere deep and glowing inside her.

And now, she meant them.

Her mind danced with an idea.

Coconut and cardamom cream puffs.

The choux dough was tricky. She'd watched and rewatched PD make it a hundred times. Boil water, melt butter, stir in flour until it forms a glossy, golden

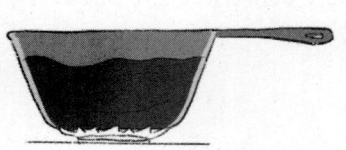

ball. Aria's arm ached as she stirred in the eggs, one by one, but she didn't stop. The dough turned smooth and silky, just as it should.

She piped tiny mounds with care, hands steady, breath even.

Into the oven.

She peeked through the glass.

They rose. Golden. Puffy. Light as clouds.

S h e spun in a silent, ridiculous victory twirl, screaming in her head. SO much screaming!

While they cooled, she whipped up a luscious coconut cream with a hint of cardamom and

sugar, filling each puff until they looked like snowballs on a tropical holiday. She toasted coconut flakes to a perfect gold and dusted the tops like falling snow.

When the judges announced her name for the first place, Aria didn't move for a second.

Then –

'AAAAAA AAAAAAAA AAAAAAAAA!'
Sarah ran through the class to hug her, sending her crashing down on the floor.

She picked Aria up, who lifted her blue ribbon high like it was a trophy from a magical land. 'THAT'S MY BEST FRIEND!' Sarah screamed, before quickly putting the remaining pastries into a box.

At home, Papa popped open fizzy orange soda like it was champagne.

Mum made popcorn. Sarah tossed cushions onto the floor and yelled, 'Best Day Ever!'

They danced to cheesy music. Ate ice cream straight from the tub. Sang songs and laughed until Aria's cheeks hurt.

On a Roll

Later that night, as the house grew quiet and the kitchen dimmed, Aria looked at the apron hanging on its hook. The sequins caught the light from the hallway, glinting softly.

She smiled.

It might be just fabric and thread to some. But Aria knew it was magic. She just knew it. And it would win her this competition.

How to make vanilla buttercream

6

Toasts, Tumbles and Torn Threads

Two wins in, Aria sure was in her element – measuring, mixing and humming a made-up baking song.

*'Flip it once, don't let it burn,
Golden sides and then you turn,
Add some jam, give it a twirl –
Baking queen, go rule the world!'*

Her hair was tied up in a messy puff, she had her apron on (her magic apron), and a streak of flour shone across her nose.

Today's breakfast menu? French toast with berry compote, whipped cream and a light dusting of vanilla sugar. Nope, a simple jam, toast just wouldn't do anymore. Not after two wins at the Big PD Bake-Off.

'Eggs are tricky, shells might fly,
But I will bake till I touch the sky!
Magic's here, I feel it swirl –
Apron on, I'm a baking girl!

She sang, flawlessly flipping a sizzling custardy slice in the pan, thinking about the macarons they had to bake for the final round.

She dramatically tossed a berry into her mouth. 'Ugh. Why can't they just invent shell-less eggs already? Macarons need so many eggs!' Despite all the success, the fear of breaking eggs still haunted the little girl.

Peanut, her not-so-trusty sous-chef, whined at her feet, nose twitching at the smell of the golden-brown French toast.

'Yes, Pea,' Aria said, reaching down to scratch his head. 'I'll give you some. No licking until I'm done, okay?'

But Peanut had other plans.

As Aria reached for the whipped cream to give it one last swish, Peanut leapt, graceful as a pancake mid-flip, but only managed to grab the edge of Aria's apron.

'Hey! No – Pea, stop!'

He tugged harder, wanting nothing more than to get all the batter stuck on the apron. And in a matter of seconds, it was chaos.

Toasts, Tumbles and Torn Threads

A rip.

A tug.

A flurry of fabric.

'PEA!' Aria shrieked, stumbling backward as the apron yanked off her neck and landed in Peanut's mouth like a trophy.

The dog sprinted off, dragging the pink apron through the house – ripping, tearing, chomping at the sticky spots where the batter had stuck to the cloth.

By the time Aria caught up to him, the apron was in pieces. A sad mess that no magic could mend.

She froze.

'No …' Aria whispered. 'No, no, no …'

The words barely escaped her lips before she dropped to her knees. Tears rushed up before she could stop them – hot and heavy and furious.

She clutched at the shredded fabric with trembling fingers, as if she could somehow stitch it back together just by holding it tighter. But the sparkly front was torn clean through.

The world seemed to slow down. The sizzling from the stove faded. The ticking clock dulled. Even the light felt different, like someone had dimmed it.

A strange hollowness settled in her chest, cold and echoey, like the moment after a balloon pops.

Footsteps pounded across the house.

'What happened?!' Mrs Mehra's voice rang out, sharp with worry as she rushed in, Mr Mehra right behind her.

Peanut looked up innocently, tongue hanging out, tail thumping, completely unaware of the destruction he'd left behind.

Aria didn't speak. She simply held up what was left of her precious apron.

Her hands trembled. Her shoulders shook. Her face crumpled.

'Oh, sweetheart …' Mrs Mehra knelt beside her, instantly wrapping her in the kind of hug that only moms could give. The kind that said, *I'm here, no matter what.*

'It's gone,' Aria choked out, burying her face in her mother's shoulder. Her voice was small, cracked, unfamiliar. 'I ruined it. And now everything is ruined. The final. The macarons. Everything.'

Mr Mehra lowered himself beside them, one arm around both the girls.

'It's just an apron, Aru,' he said gently.

'It wasn't just an apron!' Aria burst out, lifting her tear-streaked face. 'It was *everything*. My shield. My cape. Without it, I'm nothing. I'm a horrible pretend baker.'

Her voice broke again, jagged with hurt. 'You don't get it. I can't do it. I don't even want to try anymore.'

The words shocked even her as they fell out – sharp and final.

She meant them.

All the practice. All the planning. All the secret flavour tests. Gone. And now, instead of excitement, all she felt was dread. Cold and sticky, like undercooked batter.

Mr Mehra exchanged a look with his wife – one of those quiet, wordless glances parents share when they are seriously worried about their child.

'Oh, beta …' Mrs Mehra whispered, gently brushing a damp curl off Aria's cheek. 'The magic wasn't in the apron.'

'It never was,' her father added. 'It was always in you.'

'Remember when I said you have to wear your courage on the outside?' her mom said softly. 'That was just a nudge. A way to help you see what was already there.'

Aria sniffled, lashes clumped with tears, her bottom lip trembling. 'But that magic's gone now, too,' she said in a whisper. 'It left with the apron.'

'It didn't, I promise,' her mom whispered, placing a warm hand over Aria's heart. 'It's right here.'

'You're the one who made that pineapple–black pepper cheesecake,' her dad added. 'And the coconut–cardamom choux. That wasn't the apron, Aru. That was you. You chose those flavours. You mixed and piped and baked them into brilliance.'

'And the strawberry-lassi swirl cupcakes?' he said with a dramatic wave. 'That was pure Aria Mehra magic. No flour fairy or cupcake cape required.'

Aria let out a shaky breath. Her chest still ached.

'But the final's tomorrow ... and macarons are so hard ... and PD will be watching ... and now without the apron ... I CAN'T, I REALLY CAN'T—'

'You're still going to do it,' Mrs Mehra said firmly, cupping her daughter's face in both hands.

'With or without an apron. Because you've got one of the bravest hearts I've ever seen.'

'And a very big brain for flavour,' Mr Mehra added, tapping her forehead gently.

'And fingers made for piping perfection.'

'And a dog who's officially banned from apron proximity,' he added, glaring playfully at Peanut.

Peanut gave a guilty little woof and curled up beside Aria, resting his head on her knee, tail tucked in.

For a moment, they just sat there – on the floor, in the middle of the mess.

Aria blinked. The French toast was cold. The compote had turned to jam. Everything felt overdone, inedible.

'I guess – I guess we'll need a new apron,' she murmured, wiping her nose on her sleeve.

'We absolutely will,' her parents said together.

'With a bigger whisk,' Mr Mehra declared.

'And glitter,' her mom added with a wink.

'And a built-in snack pocket,' her dad grinned.

Aria let out a sigh. She knew she couldn't give up. Her parents and Sarah wouldn't let her. She'd have to do it for them. Even if it meant doing it badly.

How to seperate whites and yok

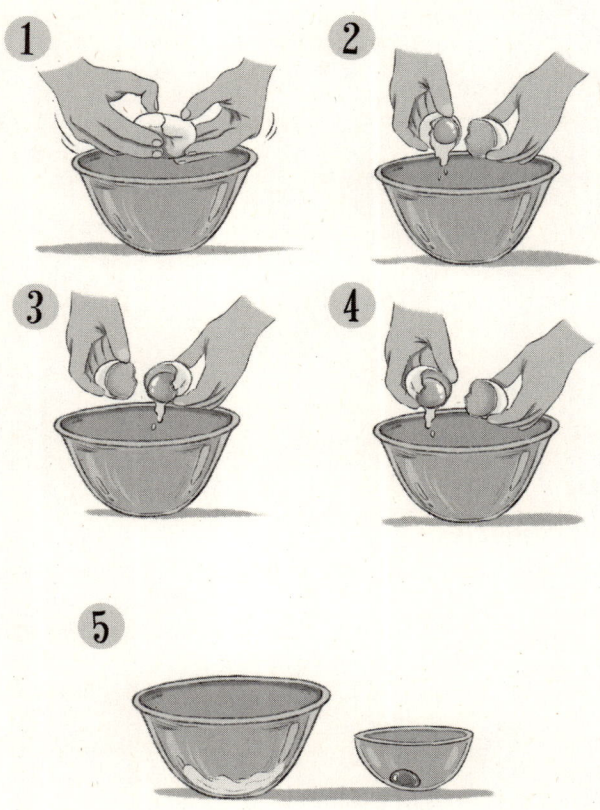

7

Shattered Shells

Aria didn't speak a word the whole car ride.

Her backpack slumped at her feet. Her fingers twisted the frayed corner of her Sprinkle Queen T-shirt, and she refused to look up. Even her curls looked sad.

'She doesn't have to go if she doesn't want to,' her mother had said in the morning.

But Sarah had other ideas.

'Oh yes, she does,' she declared. 'You really want to miss meeting Pari Doshi? Final round, Aria. Come on. I don't care if I have to carry you in on a rolling pin.'

And so, here she was – at the final round of Bake It to the Top! Junior Edition, with no magic apron and no magic in her.

The kitchen arena buzzed with excitement. Kids darted around in personalized aprons, mixers and hopes revving. PD's poster loomed large on the back wall, all sunshine and spatulas. In front stood the real PD, Miss Nanda introducing her to a round of applause.

But Aria barely looked ahead. Her eyes were glued to her station. To the eggs. Lined up like little white domes of doom.

Her stomach swirled like under-whipped cream.

She had a brilliant idea – she *knew* she did.

Classic shells filled with creamy butterscotch ganache and crushed salty banana chips with just a sprinkle of flaky salt on top. It would've been her masterpiece.

But now, without the apron …

What was the point?

'Contestants!' PD's voice rang out across the studio. 'You've got two hours. Macaron magic begins in three … two … one!'

Mixers whirred. Sifters swished. Kids squealed.

Aria cracked her first egg.

Crunch. A sliver of shell dropped into the bowl

'Ugh,' she whispered fishing with a spoon. The shard slipped

deeper into the whites like it was playing hide-and-seek with her.

Second egg. Crunch. Another shard.

'I knew it,' she muttered. 'It was all the apron. I can't do this. I *never* could.'

She could feel eyes on her. PD and Miss Nanda moving through the rows, smiling and nodding.

By the third egg, she wasn't even pretending. Her fingers were sticky. Her bowl a gloopy mess.

She tried to go on. But not too long in she couldn't ignore it anymore.

Her ganache had the texture of sand. Her shells were lopsided and deflated.

And just like that, she couldn't breathe.

The panic rose like overbeaten meringue, too fast, too high.

She bolted past Sarah's startled, 'Hey, where are you going?', past the flashing cameras of the school photography team, past a table where someone was flambéing something that absolutely should not have been on fire.

She locked herself in the bathroom stall, sat on the closed lid of the toilet and let the tears come – hot, humiliated, overwhelming.

All the wins. All the dreams. All the joy of mixing and measuring and licking batter off spoons – they felt far, far away.

She buried her face in her hands.

Then – footsteps.

A quiet knock on the door.

Then a pause.

'Hey!' a soft voice called. 'Are you okay in there?'

Aria froze. That voice was so familiar. But it couldn't be –

'I saw someone running,' the voice continued. 'Kind of looked like she'd just lost a bake-off and a best friend in one go. Thought I'd check in.'

Aria peeked through the crack in the stall.

PD stood there in jeans and a sunflower-yellow baker's coat, holding two paper towels and a half-eaten pistachio cookie.

Aria's jaw dropped. She wiped her face hastily, heart thudding.

'Y-you're …'

'Yup,' PD said, crouching down to Aria's eye level. 'And you look like someone who could use a cookie and maybe a little company.'

She extended the cookie like a peace offering.

Aria slowly opened the door. Took the cookie. Sat down on the tiled floor beside her.

'I'm sorry,' Aria mumbled. 'I just – everything's going wrong. My eggs are a disaster. My ganache is gritty. My shells look like …'

PD laughed. 'Been there. During my first show, I mixed up salt and sugar in an apple pie. Took one bite, spat it across the room, then dropped a whole bowl of dough on my foot and cried under a prep table for twenty minutes.'

Aria blinked. 'You cried?'

'Big time. Then I tripped on my apron string and landed in a mop bucket. Not my finest hour.'

'But you're *you*,' Aria said, voice cracking. 'You're like … the best.'

'Thanks,' PD smiled. 'But being the best isn't about never messing up. It's about getting back up after you do. Every time.'

Aria hugged her knees. 'I thought the apron made me special. Without it, I'm just ... me. And I'm not enough.'

'Let me tell you a secret,' PD said. '*You* are the magic. Aprons, trophies, gold mixers – they're just tools. You're the one doing the baking.'

Aria stared at her cookie. 'I don't know if I can go back out there.'

'It's scary. I get it,' PD said gently. 'But the bravest thing a baker can do is try again. Even when the shells shatter. Even when the shell sinks. Especially then.'

Aria sniffed. 'They're probably halfway through judging already.'

'Maybe,' PD shrugged. 'But maybe you've still got time. Time to show everyone what Sprinkle Queen's really made of.'

Aria looked up, the tiniest spark returning to her eyes. 'Some sort of butterscotch ganache?'

PD grinned. 'Now *that* sounds like magic.'

Aria stood slowly, still unsure. But her spine was straighter. Her fingers less shaky.

'I'm going to start over,' she said quietly.

'That's the spirit,' PD said. 'Oh, pro tip – try cracking your eggs on a flat surface instead of the bowl. Fewer shards. More control. And for the macarons, try lowering the temperature to 140°C to bake the shells. That should save you resting time.'

Aria nodded. Then, for the first time that morning, she smiled. Just a little.

'Let's go bake something brave,' PD nodded.

How to whip an egg white

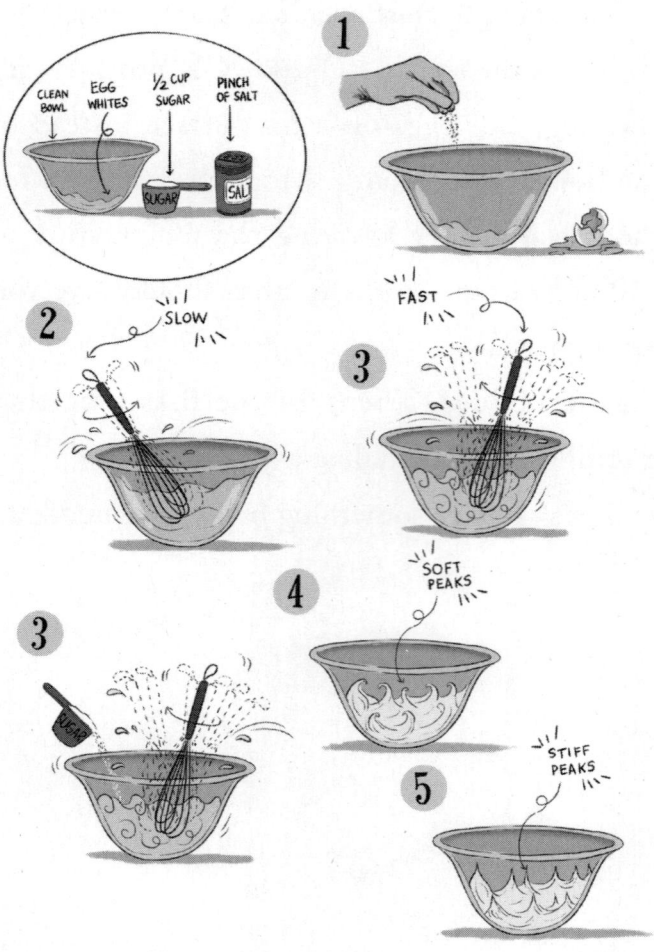

8

It Might Just Be a Comeback

Back in the baking studio, the finale was still going on.

The timer glowed red. 'You have one hour left to create your twelve showstopping macarons!' Miss Nanda announced.

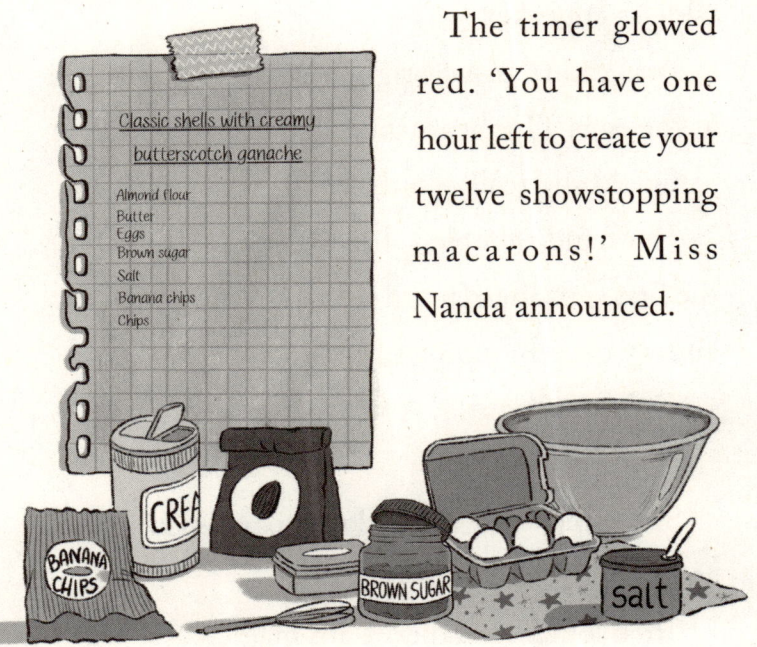

The studio surged into renewed motion. But Aria … didn't.

She hovered near her station, fingers twitching, eyes scanning the ingredients. The whirring, clanging, clattering noise of mixers and bowls felt like thunder in her ears.

Sarah nearly fainted when she saw her. *'YOU'RE BACK!'* she whisper-screamed, her eyes wide as cupcakes.

Aria didn't answer right away. She just stared at the eggs. Her heart thudded.

Could she really do this?

Her hand trembled slightly as she reached for the first egg. She glanced sideways – everyone was already deep in piping or mixing.

Then she heard it. A whisper in her mind.

'You are magic.'

She whispered it out loud, barely audible. 'I am … magic.'

Then louder, steadier. 'I am magic.'

It Might Just Be a Comeback

She cracked the first egg – flat surface, just like PD said.

No shell. She exhaled slowly.

Sarah squealed again. 'SHE'S BACK, BABY!'

The world shifted.

Aria's hands moved with more purpose. Crack. Crack. Whisk. Fold. Measure. Pour.

Each step came with more certainty. Her rhythm grew – slow at first, then stronger, faster.

Her almond flour folded into the meringue, gentle and rhythmic, exactly like PD said – *like tucking in a sleeping kitten.*

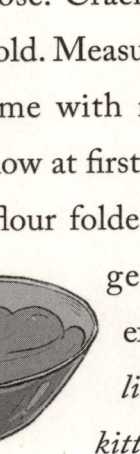

Ganache on the stove. Butter, cream, brown sugar, all melting into a liquid gold dream. She dipped her pinkie in, tasted –

'Oh! My ganache, it's good,' she whispered, a smile creeping onto her lips.

And then – the twist.

She grabbed the packet of banana chips and her rolling pin.

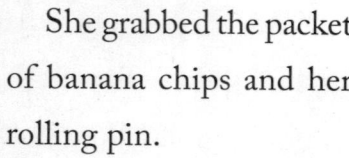

Crunch. Crunch. Crunch.

She pulverized them like a

thunder god. The salty-sweet aroma hit her like lightning. She tasted a crumb and giggled – salty, sweet and just enough chaos.

Shells piped in perfect rounds. Trays tapped on the counter like war drums. Into the oven they went.

While the macarons baked, Aria spun across her station like she was on a mission, whipping ganache, sorting shells, tapping her fingers to an invisible beat.

Oven timer: *Ding!*

Shells out. Slightly golden, perfectly risen.

Aria's breath caught in her throat.

She picked the best twelve. The champions. The ones that looked like they belonged in a magazine. Each one filled with a swirl of butterscotch ganache, a crunch of salty banana, a sparkle of flaky sea salt.

She lined them up with a flourish just as Miss Nanda called, 'Three … two … ONE! Hands up, everyone!'

Aria lifted her arms. Her cheeks were dusted with flour. Her curls bounced wild and untamed. Her eyes gleamed.

It Might Just Be a Comeback

She had done it.

The judges circled.

And then, PD stood at her table.

She looked down. Then up at Aria.

'Butterscotch and … banana chips?' she asked, intrigued.

Aria nodded, voice soft but steady. 'With sea salt. For contrast.'

PD took a bite. Chewed slowly.

Her eyes widened.

'Oh.'

She took another bite. Closed her eyes.

Then – a laugh. A big, loud, delighted laugh.

'This is *genius*! It's like banana bread's cooler, fancier cousin. The salt! The crunch! This is like a party in a patisserie!'

Aria's knees almost gave way. She stood as still as her macarons, trying to hold back the bubbling joy.

Pari turned to Miss Nanda. 'This – this is going straight into my shop. Right now. We're calling it *The Aria Special*. First of the signature range.'

Aria's jaw dropped. 'Really?'

'You bet your whisk, kid. You brought the magic.'

The room erupted.

Kids clapped. Judges beamed. Sarah screamed and hugged Aria so hard, she let out a squeak.

Aria didn't come first in the competition; the totals didn't add up in her favour. But she didn't mind. She'd got her signature in PD's patisserie anyway. And more importantly, she now *knew* –

She had her flavours.

She had her fire.

She was magic.

She was going to be the best baker in the world.